For
Mom, Dad
and
Lolly Dog.

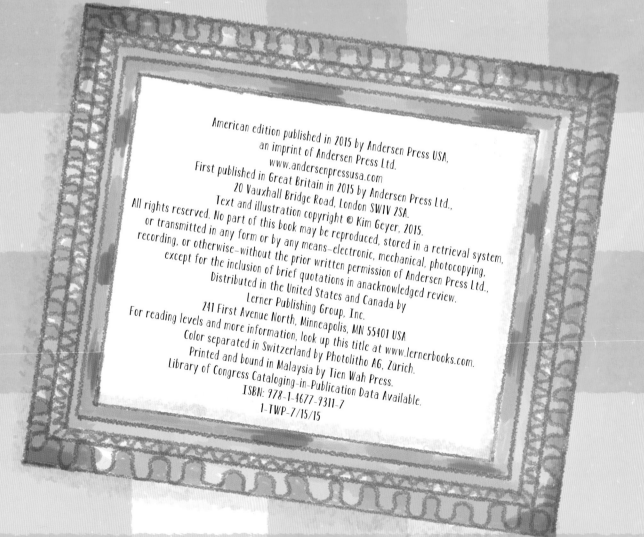

American edition published in 2015 by Andersen Press USA,
an imprint of Andersen Press Ltd.
www.andersenpressusa.com
First published in Great Britain in 2015 by Andersen Press Ltd.,
20 Vauxhall Bridge Road, London SW1V 2SA.
Text and illustration copyright © Kim Geyer, 2015.
Distributed in the United States and Canada by
Lerner Publishing Group, Inc.
241 First Avenue North, Minneapolis, MN 55401 USA
For reading levels and more information, look up this title at www.lernerbooks.com.
Color separated in Switzerland by Photolitho AG, Zurich.
Printed and bound in Malaysia by Tien Wah Press.
Library of Congress Cataloging-in-Publication Data Available.
ISBN: 978-1-4677-9311-7
1-TWP-7/15/15

Go to Sleep, Monty!

KIM GEYER

ANDERSEN PRESS

Max loved his toy dog, Snuffly Poo.
They had been together since Max was a baby.

Now that Max was a big boy,
Mom and Dad said he could have a real puppy.
"But you'll have to look after him," they said.

Max went with his parents
to choose the puppy.

He loved Monty!

Monty was big, but he was still a baby. Max tried really hard to look after him, but it wasn't easy...

"Bad boy, Monty!" "Oh, no!"

That night, Max put Monty in his very own puppy bed, and covered him with his very own puppy blanket.

"Go to **sleep, Monty,**" said Max.

But Monty did not sleep.
He whimpered and he wept.

"Now, now, don't be afraid,
Monty," said Max, tucking
him in tightly.
"Nighty, night."

But Monty did not sleep.
He scratched at the door and
he barked and he howled.

"Ok, Monty," said Max. "You can
sleep in here just for tonight."

But Monty did not sleep. He jumped on Max's bed and he slobbered and he dribbled and he drooled.

Max sang him a song,
did a little dance
and made shadow
puppets on the wall.

But still Monty did not sleep.
He went into the kitchen.

uh oh!

He howled and he hooted, and he yapped and he yelped, and he wailed and he whined, and he sniffled and he snuffled, and he...

...peed on the floor!

Max loved Monty very much, but he wished,
just a little bit, that Monty would go to sleep.
There must be something that would help.
Suddenly Max had a **brilliant idea!**

"I'll lend you Snuffly Poo, Monty," said Max.
"He always helped me go to sleep when I was a baby."
But Monty had other ideas...

"Oh, no!
Bad Monty!
Poor Snuffly Poo!"

Max carried Monty's basket back into the living room, and Monty hid under his blanket.

Then Max felt sorry. He hadn't meant to shout at Monty.

But, he was very, very sleepy now.

He yawned and rubbed his tired eyes.

Max gave Monty a big cuddle and climbed

into the puppy bed to have a think,

just for a moment, just for a while, just until ...

Max was fast asleep. "Nighty, night," thought Monty.